EDWARD
AND THE
BOOK CROOKS

To Rebecca.
Happy reading!

Diana Shaw

2010

A Quick Brown Fox Publications Book

First published in Great Britain by Quick Brown Fox in 2009.
Copyright © Diana Shaw, 2009.

Also by the same author:
Septimus Smythe And The Spectre Detectors
(ISBN 9780955480454)

ISBN-10 0955480493
ISBN-13 9780955480492

Cover Image and Illustrations © Zosia Olenska, 2009.

Cover Design and Image Editing © Chris Goodier, 2009. With
lettering and additional artwork from Nicola Stanton.

Edited by Adam Kirkman.

Quick Brown Fox Publications is an independent publisher.
Why not let them know what you thought of this book?

www.quickbrownfoxpublications.co.uk

EDWARD AND THE BOOK CROOKS

A GHOSTS OF COCKLESHORE CASTLE STORY

DIANA SHAW

ILLUSTRATIONS BY
ZOSIA OLENSKA

Quick Brown Fox Publications, 2009

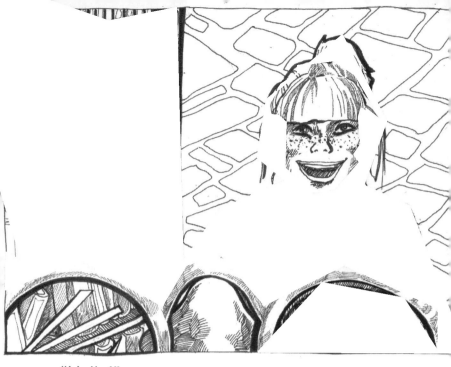

"Hello!"

Edward swung round in surprise, almost dropping the heavy book. He peered over his glasses at the fair-haired girl who was gazing up at him.

"I thought the visitors had all gone home," he remarked as he floated to the ground.

"They have. I came back to look for my book." She looked at the figure standing before her dressed in a brown jacket and knee length breeches. "Which ghost are you?" she asked.

"I'm Edward," he told her, "the castle librarian."

"I'm Hannah," she said, "and you are the fourth

ghost I have seen today!" She reached into the pocket of her jeans and took out a small red notebook and a pencil.

"I met a sailor called Horace. He was polishing a bell in the Great Hall. Then there was Septimus. He actually took off his head and put it back on again! I'm not sure who the other ghost was; she vanished before I could ask."

"Probably Mary the cook; she can be a bit shy." Edward watched as Hannah wrote down 'Mary – cook' and 'Edward – librarian.'

"Do you often come ghost hunting?" he asked. "I don't recall seeing you at the castle before."

"This is only my second time. We've just come to live in Cockleshore. Mum and Dad bought the bookshop on the high street, and my Aunty lives here. Dad isn't interested in ghosts but he likes to come to the castle to take photos. I think ghosts are great; they can do amazing tricks!" She looked up at him curiously. "You're very tall. You only had to float a little way from the ground to reach the top bookshelf!"

"I wasn't always this tall," Edward sighed. "Before I became a ghost, I was just average height for a man. Then one day, a bookcase toppled over on me. I was flattened out and stretched!"

"Wow! That must have hurt!" Hannah cringed.

"How long ago did it happen?"

"Oh, about three hundred and fifty years ago."

"How did the bookcase come to fall on you?" Hannah asked.

"It all happened when Oliver Cromwell got rid of King Charles I and made himself Lord Protector of England. The family I worked for were ordered to leave the castle. I should have gone too but I wanted to make sure the books in the library were safe, in the hope that one day the family might return. I hid the books, and not a moment too soon I might say!"

"Why? What happened?"

"Well, some of Cromwell's soldiers arrived.

They had no respect for the beautiful castle as it was then. They even stabled their horses in the library!" Edward shuddered at the memory of it.

"What did you do?" asked Hannah.

"I was so angry that I did not worry that it was just me against so many soldiers. I tried to drive them away! Laughing and waving their swords, they backed me into a corner. I bumped into an unsteady bookcase and well, you know the rest."

"But you managed to save the books."

"Yes," said Edward. "I became a ghost and the other ghosts here became my friends. Together we made a plan to get rid of the soldiers. One dark stormy night, we all gathered and used our best haunting skills to frighten the wits out of them! When Septimus removed his head that was the final straw. The soldiers fled in terror and never returned."

"Did the family ever come back?" asked Hannah.

"Sadly no," Edward said. "The castle was left, abandoned to decay over time. For many years, only we ghosts lived here. Parts of the building crumbled to ruins over the next three hundred years, but the Great Hall survived along with the library and the kitchens; and some of the bedrooms were still habitable. Eventually, the parts of the castle that remained were restored and the place became a tourist attraction. The new owner was quick to discover that the castle was haunted so we became the main attraction to visitors. These days, people call it Cockleshore Castle because it's not far from the town." He glanced at the library clock.

"Oh dear, it's almost five. You'll be locked in if you don't hurry. Now where did you put your book?"

"On a table over here, I think," said Hannah crossing the room. "Yes, here it is. I was sitting here while my dad had a look round the library."

"That looks interesting," said Edward, peering over her shoulder at the brightly coloured cover, "may I have a look?"

Edward could not resist books. He turned the first page...

"Oh!" He jumped back in alarm as something sprang up with a loud 'croak'.

Hannah laughed. "It's a novelty book," she explained. "I got it for my tenth birthday last week. There's a surprise on every page!"

"You're telling me," said Edward.

"See," Hannah said, "it's a frog on a little spring. The writing on the page is all about frogs. When I close the book, the page flattens out again. There are lots of different creatures on the other pages."

"My goodness," said Edward. "How books have changed! I'd love to have a look at the rest of it but we really must hurry."

Hannah picked up her book and they were heading for the door when Edward stopped.

"Too late!" he said as they heard the sound of a key turning in a lock and then footsteps walking away.

"Hello!" shouted Hannah.

"He will never hear you," said Edward. He thought for a moment. "There is only one thing for it," he said at last, "I will have to take you through the secret passage."

"Really? How do we get in?"

"It's a SECRET! Close your eyes and promise not to look."

"Alright." Reluctantly, Hannah did as she was told.

There was a loud click followed by a creaking sound.

"You can open them now," said Edward.

One of the large bookcases had swung away from the library wall to reveal an opening.

"Follow me," said Edward. "It's rather dark in there but just follow my ghostly glow!"

Hannah stepped through the entrance behind him. The tall, thin shape of Edward had taken on a luminous appearance. It was easy to follow him as he turned left along a short passage, rounded a corner and glided down a flight of steps.

"Here we are," said Edward. He raised his hand and seemed to touch something high up. Slowly, a section of the wall slid to one side, just enough for Hannah to step through.

They were looking out onto the side car park. Only one car remained and there was a man sitting in it with his back to them.

"That's my dad," Hannah said. "I must go, but we are coming again next Saturday. Can I see you then?"

"I'll be in the library," Edward told her.

When she reached the car, she turned to wave but the wall had slid back perfectly in place and there was no sign of Edward.

chapter two

A shaft of sunlight beaming through the window brightened the corner of the library and captured, mid-flight, the multitude of tiny dust particles. Edward rubbed vigorously with his duster as he polished away at the glass-fronted bookcase that housed the most valuable books in the library. He hummed a little tune to himself as he worked. Now and again, he would glance impatiently at the clock on the library wall.

"I wonder what time she will be here," he thought to himself as he put down his duster and floated across the room.

On such a fine day, the library was deserted. Most of the visitors were outside exploring the castle grounds.

"I suppose you'll want to go ghost hunting!" Hannah's father laughed as he took his camera from the car boot. "Well, I want some pictures of the courtyard and the main tower. Let's meet in the café one hour from now. Make sure you stay within the castle grounds!"

"Promise," said Hannah as she set off for the main door.

She walked quickly down the hallway leading to the library. The great wooden doors stood slightly ajar so she slipped through quietly and looked around; there was no sign of anyone, not even Edward.

"Good morning!"

Hannah followed the sound with her eyes in time to see Edward slowly appearing through the bookcase on the far wall.

"I don't need to open the way into the passage," he explained with a grin. "As you know, a ghost can float through anything!"

"What were you doing in there?" Hannah asked.

"Well, you remember we turned left the other day? If you turn right, you come to my secret room where I do my book repairs without any interruptions from visitors."

Hannah's eyes widened. "A secret room; will you show me?"

Edward hesitated. "Very well, but you check the hallway to make sure no-one is coming while I open the passage for you."

She peeped round the big door then called, "All clear!"

When she turned back into the room Edward was standing by the opening beckoning to her.

"Quickly!" he said.

Once inside, Hannah waited in the darkness as the bookcase swung back into place.

"Follow me," said Edward as he once again began to glow. After a short distance, the passage ended as they stopped in front of a door.

Edward glided through then turned to open the door for Hannah. She stepped inside a small dark room with no windows.

The only light came from Edward and she could just make out the shape of a table and a chair.

"How can you see to work in here?" Hannah asked.

"Candles!" Edward produced a box of matches and moments later four large flickering candles lit the room; one on the table and the others arranged on stands. There was a pile of books on the table and the tools he needed to do his repair jobs.

"Visitors are allowed to look at some of the books and, after a time, pages may come loose or bindings need reinforcing," explained Edward. "If anyone wishes to see any of the more valuable books, they must make an appointment with the castle owner and he will show them."

"Who knows about this secret room?" Hannah asked.

"Just the other ghosts and now you; you won't tell anyone, will you?"

Edward sounded a little worried as if the possibility had only just occurred to him.

"Don't worry, I won't," she reassured him.

Suddenly, a little breeze came whistling through the keyhole, extinguishing one of the candle flames in passing. It gathered like a whirlwind in a corner of the room, spinning round and round and whipping up the dust from the floor.

Hannah watched in amazement as slowly in the centre of the whirlwind a figure began to appear.

"Septimus!" cried Edward.

Hannah recognised the ghost who had performed the amazing feat of removing and replacing his head. Now Septimus, seeing Edward was not alone, raised his hat and gave a sweeping bow.

"Ah! I see you have a visitor, Edward."

"This is Hannah; she likes to hunt for ghosts. She particularly enjoys watching your special trick!" said Edward.

"Pleased to meet you, Hannah. I was beheaded on the orders of King Henry VIII, you know; that's how I am able to remove and replace my head. I would do it now for you but I'm afraid there's no time to spare. Do excuse me, but there is something I must tell Edward and it can't wait." He turned to his friend.

"Edward, there was a man in the library behaving very suspiciously. I remained invisible and watched as he fetched the library ladder. I know that only the castle owner uses the library ladder when he needs to get one of the valuable books. The man wrote something on a piece of paper before he left. He kept looking around all the time; I think he was worried about being

14

seen. I followed him outside but there was such a crowd of tourists that I lost him."

"Oh verses and volumes!" said Edward, "that does sound odd. Can you remember what he looked like?"

"His hair was ginger and he wore glasses. I thought he looked a bit scruffy actually; he had on an old black jacket and blue jeans. I'll go and warn Horace to be on the lookout."

"Right, I'll tell Mary," said Edward.

Septimus bowed to Hannah. "See you later!" he told Edward and then he vanished.

"I had better get along to the kitchen," Edward said.

"And I suppose my Dad will be looking for me," said Hannah, looking at her watch. "I'm not sure when we will be coming to the castle again but I've had an idea. Why don't you come to see me at the bookshop one day?"

Edward smiled. "I'd like that. How about Wednesday afternoon, when the castle is closed to visitors?"

"That's great. It's half term so I will be on holiday from school. I'll be watching out for you."

They had reached the end of the passage. Edward made sure that no-one was around then he let Hannah out.

"Right, I shall make myself invisible; no time to entertain the visitors just now. See you Wednesday!" With that, he rose from the ground and vanished.

Edward glided invisibly along the middle of Cockleshore high street. He floated above the traffic, his eyes searching left and right for the bookshop.

"Ah! There it is," he said to himself and he landed neatly on the pavement right outside.

He stood for a few minutes enjoying the window display. There were dozens of books of all sizes, many with eye-catching, colourful covers. He was particularly taken with the children's books. In a few days, it would be Halloween and so the theme for the display was witches and ghosts!

A very ugly witch with a large wart on the end of her nose was suspended on a broomstick, silhouetted against a moonlit sky. She flew above a ruined castle where ghostly figures could be seen weaving in and out of the crumbling walls. The books on sale all reflected the theme: chilling, spooky volumes of stories and poems with creepy designs on the covers. Edward chuckled.

"What fun!" he thought.

He glided into the shop behind a woman and a little blond boy, and then stopped short in amazement. To Edward it was like entering a treasure trove: everywhere he looked, he could see shelves and shelves of books. He wove his way in and out around the shelves reading the labels. There were books on every subject imaginable and storybooks to suit all ages.

He reached the children's section. The little blond boy was already settled on a chair enjoying a picture book while his mother looked around the shop. There was a stand with a selection of spooky books for Halloween, just like the ones on display in the window.

Edward chose a ghost story with a particularly creepy picture on the cover and settled down in a quiet corner. The story turned out to be full of comical incidents illustrated with very funny black and white drawings. Edward couldn't suppress a chuckle. The little boy swung round at the sound but, of course, could see no one. Another chuckle, this time louder, sent him scuttling from his seat.

"Mum! Mum, there's a funny noise in the children's bit!"

His mother came over to investigate just as Edward burst into loud laughter! Grabbing her son's hand, she hurried to the counter.

"There's something very odd going on in the children's section," she told Hannah's mum in a shaky voice. "I can hear someone laughing but there's nobody there!"

Just at that moment, Hannah appeared from round a bookcase.

"I'll look, Mum," she said. "There were some children in a few minutes ago. They've probably left one of those novelty books open." Before anyone could say anything, she hurried across the shop to the children's section.

"Edward!" she whispered urgently, "Edward, is that you?"

"Oh!" Deeply absorbed in his book, Edward was completely unaware of all the fuss. "Oh, Hannah!" he cried.

"I thought it must be you," she whispered. "You've caused a right fuss. Customers could hear you laughing! Now please keep absolutely quiet until I give a signal, then follow me." She picked up a novelty book with the title 'The Laughing Policeman'.

Edward watched her return to the counter where several customers had gathered to find out what was going on. When Hannah demonstrated the book, everyone laughed. Mystery solved, the calm of the bookshop was restored.

Now Hannah made her way to a door with a sign that read 'Private – Staff Only.' She glanced all around, and then, when she was sure no-one was looking, she beckoned urgently towards the children's section. Edward needed no second bidding; he whizzed across the shop and followed her through the doorway and up a flight of stairs. Hannah led him into a little room piled high with boxes.

"Oh, what a relief!" said Edward as he slowly materialised. "Staying invisible for a long time makes a ghost tired. Sorry for causing trouble back there. I was quite carried away by that funny book!"

Hannah giggled. "Good job I managed to convince everybody that it was the novelty book making the noise," she said.

Edward looked around. "Are all these boxes full of books?" he asked.

"Yes," Hannah said. "Dad's gone to the

wholesaler to buy more books and I promised to unpack these books and arrange them on those shelves over there ready to replace any stock we sell in the shop."

"I expect you must be feeling tired," Edward said, "piles of books are heavy to carry around." He thought for a moment.

"I have an idea that could help," he said. "You empty that box of books onto the floor and I will do the rest."

Hannah began to unpack the box. Edward appeared to be doing nothing. He just sat on a chair and watched. In fact, she began to feel a bit cross. But suddenly, before she could say anything, a pile of books rose from the floor and floated across to the shelf.

"Wow!" Hannah exclaimed. "How did you do that?"

"Telekinesis," he said. "Most ghosts can do it, and some of us are pretty good at. I just think very hard about something I want to move. If I do it right, the

object moves without me even having to touch it!"

"That's a very useful trick," said Hannah. "We'll have the job done in no time!"

Before long, the books were all arranged neatly in rows on the shelves and Hannah sat in the middle of the floor surrounded by empty boxes.

"That was brilliant," she laughed.

"Glad to be of help," Edward said. He delved into his breast pocket and took out a watch attached to a gold chain. "My goodness. It's almost teatime; Mary doesn't take kindly to latecomers. I'd better go."

"We'll be coming to the castle again soon," Hannah promised.

Edward stood up and slowly disappeared.

"I'll lead the way," said Hannah.

They reached the bottom of the stairs and stepped through the doorway into the shop. There was just one customer at the counter.

Hannah felt Edward's cold breath as he whispered in her ear.

"Look! Could that be the man Septimus described?"

Hannah looked at the man with the ginger hair and dark rimmed glasses. He took a crumpled piece of paper from his pocket and showed it to Hannah's mum who looked at it and shook her head. Hannah did not speak until they were outside on the pavement.

"I think you could be right, Edward. I will try to find out what he is up to. Is there any way I can get in touch with you?"

"I know!" said Edward. "Phone the tourist office at the castle tonight, but wait until seven o'clock when we can be sure the owner has gone home. I have a funny feeling that man is up to no good!"

"Hello, is that Edward?"

Hannah had sneaked upstairs to use her mobile phone whilst her parents were watching television.

"Hello Hannah, Edward here. Did you manage to find out anything?"

"I heard Mum telling Dad that a man had been asking if she knew anything about collectors who would be interested in buying old books. Mum told him to come back tomorrow when Dad will be in the shop."

"Hmm... I wonder why he wants to know. Please try to find out what is going on."

"Don't worry. I'll make sure I'm around when he comes in. Can you be at the phone same time tomorrow night?"

"I'll be waiting for your call."

Edward put down the phone and headed for the library, deep in thought. Why had this man been using the library ladder? Had he been looking at the books in the special bookcase? If so, why hadn't he asked the owner to show him like the other visitors always did?

The moon cast its ghostly light through the library windows. Edward glided up to the glass-fronted bookcase and peered in.

There were six valuable books stored inside so the door was always kept locked. The owner of the castle kept the key in the safe in his office, only taking it out if a visitor made a special request to view the books. Edward knew that they were very special books; some of the earliest printed books in existence. He strained his eyes to read the titles.

"I wonder what that man is up to?" he thought.

He was still puzzling it over at cocoa time.

"You're very quiet tonight, Edward," Septimus remarked. "Is everything alright?"

"I'm not sure," said Edward. "Remember the man you told me about? Well, I think you could be right; he's up to no good. We must all be vigilant and report anything suspicious that happens!"

It was just after lunch on the next day. Edward had been busy all morning entertaining visitors. He could not count how many times he had glided through a bookcase and reappeared on the other side of the room. He had had great fun standing behind visitors who were reading books. He would make the pages turn, apparently on their own, much to the fright of the readers!

It was quieter in the library now. Invisible, he sat down in his favourite corner, resting his head against the back of one of the big leather armchairs.

He felt a bit sleepy... No! He mustn't doze off! He must keep alert. From here, he could observe all the goings on in the library. Just then, the great door creaked as the castle owner entered followed by a tall, rather studious-looking woman.

She sat at a table while the owner put on special white gloves, then placed the ladder in front of the glass-fronted bookcase and climbed up. He unlocked the door and lifted down one of the precious books from the top shelf. The woman, who was also wearing white gloves,

looked excited when he placed it in front of her, and she began to turn the pages.

"A magnificent example!" she praised, marvelling at the beautiful and detailed illustrations. "Thank you so much for allowing me to see it."

When the castle owner eventually replaced the book safely in the bookcase, the woman remained behind in the library, saying she would like to look around.

"Nothing unusual about that," Edward thought; he was beginning to lose interest. Apart from the woman, there were just two other browsers.

Edward was about to sneak off to the kitchen for a cup of tea from Mary when the woman caught his attention again. She suddenly strode over to the history section, quickly selected a book, and then sat down at a table. She turned the pages until she found the one she wanted. Curiously, Edward peered over her shoulder.

"The Gunpowder Plot," he thought to himself. "Nothing strange about being interested in that, I suppose." He drifted away and continued to watch her.

Now the woman took a pen and a piece of paper from her handbag. She seemed to be making notes.

"This is all rather boring," thought Edward.

"Perhaps I will slip off to the kitchen for that cup of tea."

He was about to leave when he noticed that the woman had finished writing. Then she did a very odd thing. Instead of putting the paper in her handbag, she carefully placed the page of notes inside the book, marking the page she had been reading! She replaced the book on the shelf and quickly left the library.

"How strange!" Edward thought.

He could not wait to read the paper. With trembling hands, he removed the book from the shelf and retreated to the privacy of his secret room.

The candles flickered as he sat down at his work-table and opened the book. He looked at the paper and immediately felt disappointed; there were just two lists of numbers written there.

"Verses and volumes! Whatever could this mean?" he said aloud. No words, just numbers; it was not as simple as he had hoped.

For a while, he sat puzzling. There was one number on its own at the top of the sheet. It matched the page number. That seemed straightforward enough; if the paper fell out, the correct page could easily be found again.

But all these other numbers, arranged in two

columns – what could they mean? They must have something to do with what was written on the page.

He was still puzzling when the sound of a distant buzzer distracted him. It warned visitors that it was almost time for the castle to close and he had jobs he must do in the library!

Quickly, he made up his mind what he should do. Taking his pen and a sheet of paper, he copied down the numbers. He replaced the woman's notes where he had found them and returned the book to its place in the library. One thing was certain; the paper had been left there deliberately, probably for someone else to read.

Edward had two tasks now; he must watch out for anyone selecting that book and he must try to work out the number puzzle. Just in case the paper was taken from the book when he wasn't looking, he now had his own copy of the numbers to work on when no-one was around.

Edward could not wait to speak to Hannah that evening. He was in the office well before the clock struck seven, but it was almost a quarter past when the phone rang.

"Sorry, Edward, we had tea late and I've only just managed to sneak upstairs! Anyway, I have some news. The man came back. He asked my dad about an old book he wanted to sell. Dad had obviously heard of the book. He told the man that he was sure a collector would be prepared to pay a lot of money for it, but he could not help."

"Hmm... this gets more and more interesting. Well, I have some news too." Edward told her all about the woman and the numbers on the paper.

"That sounds very mysterious. Now we have two suspicious characters; whatever is going on? I can't wait to see the paper. We might be

CHAPTER FIVE able to puzzle it out together. I've persuaded Mum to bring me to the castle tomorrow to buy tickets for the firework display. I'll try to get to see you."

"Good," said Edward. "I'll watch out for you."

He put down the phone and was about to leave the office when he noticed the photocopier. He had seen the castle owner use it many a time and it gave him an idea. If he could make a copy of the page in the book, he would be able to work on the puzzle at any spare moment and leave the book in place! He sped off to the library.

Edward was too tired to work on the puzzle that night. He carefully placed his photocopy with the list of numbers and went to bed.

Hannah couldn't think what to do. They had bought the tickets and were heading back across the car park and there had been no opportunity to see Edward. Then there came a stroke of luck!

"Look, Mum. Isn't that Aunty Sue?"

Minutes later, her mum and her aunty were agreeing to have coffee in the castle café.

"May I have a look around whilst you are chatting?" Hannah asked hopefully.

"Alright, but no more than half an hour, then we really must go."

She almost ran to the library as she was so relieved to get away.

Edward was sitting in the corner doing some invisible surveillance when she entered. He glided over and whispered in her ear. She almost shouted out in surprise when she felt his cold breath!

"Thank goodness you've come," he said, sounding excited. "Look who's over there sitting at the table near the window!"

"Oh," said Hannah, "it's him!"

Sure enough, the ginger-haired man was seated at a table studying a book.

"Can't talk here," whispered Edward urgently. "Go and stand near the bookcase in front of the secret passage. When no-one is looking, I'll open the passage just enough for you to slip through."

Minutes later, Edward materialised before Hannah in his hidden workroom.

"That man!" he said excitedly. "He has the book with the paper hidden inside. He must be working together with that woman! I've been watching him and I think I have an idea about the puzzle."

He placed the puzzle paper on the table with the photocopy of the page alongside.

"See. There are two columns of numbers. I saw him count down and then across the page. I think it may be down so many to find the line..."

"Then across to find a word!" cried Hannah gleefully.

"Precisely!" declared Edward. "Let's try!"

He read out the top number from the first column and Hannah counted down six lines.

"Now, across three and the word is..."

"Perfect!" said Hannah.

Edward wrote it down. Soon they had: 'perfect will proceed with plot November 5th meet at tower door 1605'

"Well," said Edward, scratching his head, "it all seems to make sense apart from the last bit. They are going to meet up to do something on November the fifth but how can it be in sixteen hundred and five? That was hundreds of years ago!"

Hannah thought for a moment then cried out in excitement, "I know, it's not a year, it's a time! We've been doing it at school. It's called the twenty-four hour clock and it's used for timetables so people don't confuse morning with afternoon. Instead of having to say 'am' or 'pm' you just carry on counting after twelve noon. You say thirteen, fourteen and so on. Four o'clock would be 'four' before noon and 'sixteen' after noon, so '1605' means five minutes past four in the afternoon. I suppose it was the nearest she could get to an exact hour like four o'clock, using the code with the book."

"Verses and volumes! Well done!" said Edward. "So the man and woman plan to meet by the tower door at five minutes past four on the afternoon of November 5th! But what will they do there?"

Edward and Hannah sat in silence for a second.

"I am worried that they are showing far too much interest in one of our most valuable books!"

"You don't think they are planning to try and steal it, do you?" asked Hannah in alarm.

"I don't like the sound of this," Edward said. "It will be up to us to try and stop them!"

"Well, Mum's just bought tickets for the bonfire party, so I will be here. Oh no!" said Hannah. "Mum! I had better go now, she will be wondering where I am."

Edward led the way back along the passage.

"Wait while I see if the coast is clear," he said as he made himself invisible.

As Hannah stepped through into the library, she could see they were alone. Edward materialised again and glided across to the shelf where the history books were kept. He found the book the man had been looking at and checked for the piece of paper.

"It's gone," he said. "Now it is up to us to make sure that their plan, whatever it is, does not succeed!"

"In the meantime, we can keep in touch by telephone and make our plans!" said Hannah as she started to run to the café.

"Agreed!" shouted Edward after her, and with that, he vanished.

It was Halloween and the ghosts of Cockleshore Castle were getting ready for their annual Halloween Party. Mary had prepared quite a feast and everyone was impatient for the castle owner to lock up and go home. At exactly six-thirty, they would all meet in the Great Hall and the fun would begin.

Just a few miles away, Hannah was dressing in her witch's outfit ready to join her friends to go trick or treating, but for days now all she had thought about was what would happen on Bonfire Night.

"Hannah! Time to go," her mum called up to her.

She ran down to join her friends. Tomorrow night she would phone Edward and they would make their final plans.

Meanwhile, Edward and Septimus were waiting for the other ghosts to arrive and nibbling on devilled chicken and sipping delicious fruit punch.

"So it sounds as if I was correct. I was suspicious from the moment I first saw him," said Septimus. "Whatever it is they plan to do, we will all help you stop them. Let's see what the other ghosts think at the party. I'm sure someone will have a good idea!"

"Hannah will help too," said Edward. "I'm speaking to her tomorrow so I can tell her what we've decided."

It was tradition on Halloween for each ghost to describe his or her most successful haunting experiences of the past year. It was fun entertaining the 'believers' but the best subjects were the sceptics who said they did not believe in ghosts. Scaring them was most satisfying!

"Ghosts at the castle? It's just a gimmick," they

would say. "They are just people dressed up. As for the tricks they do, all very clever but... well, they must use mirrors or something."

Septimus, of course had a great advantage. His ultimate trick was removing his head and, if all else failed, that was bound to succeed. Edward, on the other hand, was the star performer when it came to telekinesis. Now, in the eerie, flickering light of the candlelit hall he told his story.

"It happened a few weeks ago. I didn't like the young man who came into the library," he said. "He had no respect for books at all! You should have seen how roughly he turned the pages. Well, I made myself invisible and crept up behind him in the quiet corner where he was sitting. He was just about to turn a page when I made the book rise a little way from the table then float down again. At first, he must have thought he had imagined it and would have carried on reading, but when the book suddenly rose up again, and began to spin round and round his head, he leapt up with a cry and ran for the door. I took great delight in making the book follow him right across the room!"

The stories continued until everyone had taken their turn.

"Spooks and spectres!" said Septimus. "We've

had so much fun tonight that we forgot all about Edward's mysterious guests. Edward?"

Edward rose from his seat and turned to face the other ghosts. There was silence in the room as he described the events of the past few days.

"However," he concluded, "hearing all your stories tonight has given me an idea. With your help, these people can be stopped. Please listen carefully while I tell you my plan then you can add your ideas!"

The next day Edward was very busy. Invisible, he stood before the notice board in the office and made a mental note of the arrangements for the Bonfire Night celebrations. Next, he spent some time looking round the exhibition in the room adjoining the Great Hall. Tableaux showed events from history and in each scene, models were dressed in the costumes of the time. This time, Edward had his notebook with him and he made many jottings as he went round.

"Right," he said to himself when he had finished. "I will call a meeting tonight to make sure that everyone knows what to do." He glided off to his secret room where he sat for a while reading his notes.

Hannah's part in the proceedings would be vital. Edward could hardly wait until seven o'clock; he was impatient to tell her the plan.

Hannah switched off her phone, finished noting down what Edward had said in her notebook, placed it under her pillow and then went downstairs.

"Mum," she said casually, "there's a children's bonfire tea at the castle on Saturday before the firework display. May I go?"

Her mother looked at the flyer pinned to the kitchen notice board.

"I can't see why not. It begins at four. I'll drop you off then we will come back at six for the fireworks."

"Thanks," said Hannah. She felt really pleased, for things were working out just as she and Edward had planned. It would be easy to slip away from the party.

Later that evening, she sat up in bed and took her notebook from under her pillow. She ticked 'bonfire tea.'

"Mustn't forget to charge my phone," she thought, underlining that note. She thought about her conversation with Edward and smiled to herself. This was going to be fun as well as exciting. She hadn't enjoyed herself so much in ages!

Back at the castle, the meeting was underway. Edward carefully explained the final plans, while Septimus checked the office diary.

The castle owner only met up with the ghosts once a year. In the meantime, so long as they did their jobs, he was happy. However, it was handy to know of any plans he had for events at the castle in advance, so the ghosts were always prepared. Septimus took it upon himself to check the diary every night. He returned to the hall just as Edward was summing up.

"Any questions?" Edward asked. There were none.

"Right then; those two had better watch out!" He turned to Septimus.

"Anything to report?" he asked.

"Well yes, actually. I've discovered that the owner plans to lock up early on Saturday: four thirty. Only the café will remain open for the children's party. After six, everyone will be outside at the bonfire."

"That is useful," Edward said. "Very useful!"

CHAPTER
SEVEN

The ginger-haired man was pacing up and down looking at his watch. It was almost twenty past four.

"You're late!" he grumbled to the woman.

"Sorry, not my fault; the taxi was late!"

"I've left the car in the far corner of the side car park for a quick getaway," he said, ignoring her remark. "Let's get on with it!"

He opened the door to the tower room and they stepped inside. The afternoon light was fading fast and the only light in the room came through four small windows high up in the curved wall.

"It's creepy," said the woman looking round anxiously. "The taxi driver told me the castle is haunted!"

"Don't be stupid, Tracey," said Ginger crossly. "There's no such thing as ghosts. Now keep quiet and follow me."

"And it's cold in here," she complained as a sudden icy draught made her shiver.

An invisible Septimus, gliding past, chuckled to himself.

"Of course it's cold and draughty," said Ginger. "This is a castle, hundreds of years old! What do you expect: central heating? Now, stop moaning and just think about why we are here! Think of the prize!"

Septimus reached the library ahead of them, in time to report to Edward.

"They're coming," he said, "and I've seen the owner on his rounds with the keys."

"Good," said Edward. "You know what to do now."

Septimus glided out of the library into the next room.

Invisible, Edward waited quietly in the corner, facing the glass-fronted bookcase. Moments later, the door opened with a loud creak and the two intruders stepped into the library.

Ginger looked around. Satisfied that all the visitors had left, he turned to Tracey.

"The ladder," he said shortly. Together they pushed the ladder in position and Ginger began to climb.

At the same moment, hiding by the round tower in the gathering darkness, Hannah heard a voice whisper in her ear.

"It's time," said Maisie. The little kitchen maid – the youngest ghost of all – glided off back to the kitchen to report to Mary.

With trembling hands, Hannah switched on her phone and typed the number.

Ginger stopped level with the glass door and peered in. He rubbed his hands in delight and greed as he saw the books lined up. There was the one they had come for; the most valuable book on the shelf.

Taking a screwdriver from his pocket, he forced it into the slim gap between the locked doors. He pushed and twisted until the lock gave way with a splintering sound and the doors swung open. He waited a moment, holding his breath – he knew there were alarms in the castle, but had been relying on the owner not setting them until he left for the night. Fortunately, he was right. Had the alarm gone off, they would have really had to run for it!

He thrust his hand into the bookcase and grabbed the book. The beauty and quality of the leather-bound volume meant nothing to him. Pound signs danced before his eyes as he thought only of the fortune it would bring.

"Hurry up!" whispered Tracey urgently as she looked anxiously around.

Ginger began to climb down, clutching the book in his left hand and holding on with his right.

Just then, he almost lost his balance as the steps gave a shudder and shifted a few feet across the floor.

"Whoa! What's happening?" Ginger cried out in alarm as Tracey leapt out of the way. He clung on desperately as the steps lifted a

little way off the floor and began to float along. Then, suddenly, they came down to earth with a bump, forcing him to let go and jump down the last two steps. His face was as white as a sheet and he couldn't stop shaking.

"I d...don't like this," he said weakly. "Let's get out of here!"

From his dark corner, Edward watched in glee.

"I t...told you the place is haunted," stuttered Tracey as together they ran back to the tower room. Ginger reached the door to the outside first. He pulled at the handle in vain.

"It's locked!" he cried. "We'll have to find another way out!"

He turned, almost colliding with Tracey, who was right on his heels. Together, they raced back to the library and looked around. There were two other doors leading off. They knew that one led to the café and the office; there would be too many people around there. They would have to try the other door.

Ginger looked at his watch; it was ten minutes to five. He opened the door and peered into the room. It was quite dark outside now but some light from the lamps fringing the side car park shone in through the windows on the far wall. Tracey peered over Ginger's shoulder.

"What's in there?" she asked.

They stared at the odd shapes silhouetted against light from the car park lamps.

"They look like people," said Tracey, trembling. "What is this room?"

"I know," Ginger said suddenly. "It's the exhibition room. They're just models. Come on, there's a way out at the far end; should lead onto the side car park with a bit of luck!"

Looking neither right nor left, they hurried along the central aisle heading for the door. This time, Tracey grabbed the handle first.

"Oh no!" she cried. "This is locked too!"

"Let me try," said Ginger. He pulled then pushed as hard as he could but it was no use. He looked around desperately.

"There's nothing else for it, we'll have to try and sneak out past the café. There's a kids' party going on. But with a bit of luck, we won't be noticed."

"I don't like it in here," whimpered Tracey, hanging back. "We're not having much luck!"

"Oh, come on, we must hurry." Ginger looked on the wall near the door. "Look, there's a switch here, a bit of light would help!"

He flicked the switch. There was no main light, but small footlights shining up from the floor instantly illuminated the tableaux.

"That's a bit better. Now come on!" Ginger set off with Tracey a few steps behind.

Little did they know that Edward was hiding in a corner of the room watching their every move.

He chuckled to himself. They had no idea what he had in store for them. The best was yet to come!

CHAPTER EIGHT

"Stop humming! It sounds creepy."

"I'm not!"

Tracey grabbed Ginger's arm and pulled him back.

"Listen. Can't you hear it?" Her voice was shaking. "It sounds like the sailors' hornpipe!"

"I can't hear anything," said Ginger impatiently. Tracey clung to Ginger's arm.

"Listen. It's coming from over there," she said, pointing.

The tableau was a sailing scene from Tudor times. It showed a sailing ship with the crew at work. One sailor was high in the crow's nest peering through his spyglass. Another was swabbing the decks. But it was the one leaning on a crutch who caught their attention. He seemed to be staring right at them through his one good eye, while his other was covered by a patch. Dangling from his ears were gold hoops and his black hair was plaited in a pigtail down his back. He was dressed in a striped jersey and navy breeches.

Softly, the humming began again then suddenly Horace the ghostly sailor smiled a spooky smile, rose up from the deck and glided slowly towards them.

Tracey screamed and ran off down one of the side aisles. Ginger tried to follow her but, thrusting his crutch forward, Horace tripped him up and sent him sprawling! Then the sailor swiftly disappeared, tipping his hat towards Ginger in an unmistakeably terrifying manner.

Ginger scrambled to his feet, still clutching the precious book, and caught up with Tracey who had come to an abrupt halt at the end of the aisle.

She was staring at the tableau now in front of her which showed a model representing King Charles I. He knelt with his head resting on a block. Above him towered the figure of an executioner, axe poised, ready to do the dreadful deed.

"Let's get out of here," said Ginger, taking her by the arm.

Just then, from behind the executioner stepped a man dressed in doublet and hose and wearing a hat with a large feather. Tracey and Ginger trembled in terror, and stared open mouthed as the figure calmly removed his head and then tucked it under his arm! As Septimus stepped towards them, he laughed his creepiest laugh and the two would-be thieves turned and fled, screaming, towards the library.

The final tableau before the exit showed a scene from a kitchen long ago. A woman in a grey dress and white apron stood poised over

a cooking pot. Just as they drew level with her, she suddenly stepped forward, ladle in hand.

"Soup?" she enquired.

"Ahh! Let me through!" cried Ginger, battling with Tracey to be the first to escape.

For a moment, the two of them were pinned together in the doorway, pushing and shoving.

"Out of my way!" screamed Tracey, digging her elbow into Ginger's ribs.

"Ouch!" he cried as she managed to step through first.

They made for the exit leading to the café. Suddenly, a tall thin figure slowly materialised before them barring their way! Edward stretched out his hand.

"The book," he moaned. "Give me the book!"

"Not likely!" said Ginger clinging to the precious volume. He looked around, desperate to escape.

"Where can we go?" wailed Tracey.

Then they noticed the opening to the passage.

Edward had moved the bookcase and placed candles inside the secret way. To Ginger and Tracey it looked like a doorway leading to another room and hopefully, another way out. As they ran towards it, Edward glided silently and invisibly along behind them. The moment

they stepped through into the passage, he moved the bookcase back into place, trapping the two inside! Next, he passed through the wall and he materialised again between the thieves and his secret room.

"The book!" Edward shouted, extending both hands for it, using his telekinesis to make all the candles shake.

There was only one way to run now.

"Come on, Tracey!" shouted Ginger.

Guided only by the dim light from the flickering candles, Ginger stumbled down the short passage and round the corner. Suddenly, there were no more candles and in the darkness, the ground vanished beneath his feet. He landed in a heap at the bottom of the steps.

"Watch out!"

His warning came too late as, with a frightened cry, Tracey tumbled down on top of him!

"Let me up!" he grumbled, pushing Tracey off and struggling to his feet. "And be careful with the book!"

"I wish I'd never agreed to help you," Tracey shouted angrily as she tried to stand up in the darkness. "Just look at the mess we're in now! This is a dead end!"

"We'll just have to try to find our way back," said Ginger desperately.

At that moment, Edward, hovering invisibly above their heads, reached out and touched something high on the wall. The section of wall began to slide across revealing the opening leading out to the side car park.

"Look! We're free!" Ginger stepped through, leaving Tracey still on her hands and knees in the darkness. Now she managed to scramble to her feet and stumble after him.

"We made it!" she cried.

"The car's over there, follow me!" Ginger set off with Tracey close behind.

"NOT SO FAST!"

It all happened in seconds. A blinding bright light shining straight into their eyes made them stop in their tracks. Ginger felt a hand on his shoulder.

"I'll take that," said a voice.

As the dazzling colours cleared from in front of his eyes, he found himself staring into the face of a police officer. By the glaring light of the car headlights, he could see people standing all around. No fight left in him, Ginger meekly handed over the precious book.

"All that and for nothing," Tracey grumbled as she was led towards the waiting police car.

Behind them, the secret panel quietly slid back into place. Edward rubbed his hands together and chuckled with glee as he made his way back to the library where the other ghosts were waiting for him.

"That was the best fun I've had in ages!" Horace said.

"Me too," said Septimus. "I've never seen anyone look so scared."

"Yes," Edward chuckled. "Everything went perfectly. I think those two will be sleeping with the light on for a long time to come!"

Just then, there was a loud bang from outside. All the ghosts jumped!

"Goodness! What was that?" asked Edward.

"A firework," Mary answered. "It's gone six o'clock. Come on – if we hurry, we'll be able to catch the rest of the fireworks!"

Down in the courtyard, Hannah stood with her parents watching the fireworks scatter into the night sky. As a volley of rockets exploded in a mass of bright multi-coloured stars, she looked up at the tower windows where she was sure her friends would be watching.

CHAPTER NINE

"Hannah! Where have you been?"

"Sorry Edward, I've been dying to come all week but school started again on Monday."

"Never mind, it has been so busy here I have hardly had a minute to spare! A man came to repair the bookcase and he fitted a special alarm that's always on. If anyone tampers with the glass doors, we will know straight away! There have been more visitors than usual too; everyone wants to see the scene of the crime!"

Just then, as if to prove the point, a crowd of visitors entered the library.

"Oh dear, we can't talk here," said Edward. "Watch out for my signal and come through to the secret room."

Hannah stood quietly in the corner where she had found her friend busily tidying the bookshelves. When Edward was satisfied that no-one was looking, he carefully opened the way to the passage then raised his hand and beckoned her. Moments later, she was sitting on the little footstool in Edward's workshop watching as he lit the candles.

"It worked, Hannah!" he was saying. "We stopped them, didn't we? Everyone did their bit and it worked!"

"I saw their faces as the police took them away," laughed Hannah. "I think you must have given them a very scary time!"

Edward told her how each ghost had done their bit to frighten the wits out of the crooks.

"As soon as Maisie told Mary that you had phoned the police, we got to work. We were determined to make them suffer!"

Suddenly, a little breeze came whistling through the keyhole. It gathered like a whirlwind in a corner of the room, spinning round and round and whipping up the dust from the floor.

"Hello, Septimus!" laughed Hannah.

"However did you guess it was me?" chuckled Septimus as, beginning with his head, he slowly materialised.

"We were just talking about the events of last Saturday," said Edward.

"Wasn't it fun; and just look at this! Someone left it behind in the café!"

COCKLESHORE
guardian

CROOKS SPOOKED AT THE CASTLE!

"Anyone who does not believe in ghosts should think twice," says Mike Mason, known in criminal circles as Ging-er. The would-be book thief is still shaking at the thought of his spooky experience at Cockleshore Castle. In fact, he says he would rather remain in prison than go there ever again!

On the eveni-ng of 5th Nove-mber, Mason and his accomp-lice Tracey Crossley set out to steal a very valuable book from the castle library.

Septimus lifted his hat, which took his whole head with it. He sighed and pulled a face at Hannah, making her laugh, and then pulled the hat from his head.

Septimus then took a folded page of newspaper from the hat and replaced the hat on his head and then his head on his neck. Curious, Hannah and Edward gathered round as he spread out the page on the table.

"There's even a photograph of the thieves being led away," he said pointing to the article at the top of the page.

CROOKS SPOOKED AT THE CASTLE!

Hannah started to read aloud.

"Anyone who does not believe in ghosts should think twice," says Mike Mason, known in criminal circles as Ginger. The would-be book thief is still shaking at the thought of his spooky experience at Cockleshore Castle. In fact, he says he would rather remain in prison than go there ever again!

On the evening of 5th November, Mason and his accomplice Tracey Crossley set out to steal a very valuable book from the castle library. Quick-thinking Hannah Browne, whose father owns the bookshop on Cockleshore high street, phoned the police when she noticed the pair behaving suspiciously.

When interviewed at the police station, both Mason and Crossley stated that had it not been for the ghosts they believe they would have succeeded. It could be some time before the two of them recover from their spooky experience; in fact, they have both asked if the officer will leave the lights on in their cells at night, as they are too frightened to go to sleep in the dark!

I asked Hannah Browne whether she believes in ghosts. "Oh yes," she said, "I often go ghost hunting at the castle and I have seen several of the ghosts who live there."

Well, whatever you believe, some things remain unexplained.

How did the thieves get out of the castle onto the car park? Many people have searched for the door, but reached the puzzling conclusion that it does not exist!

What do you, our readers, think about ghosts? Please write with your opinions to: editor@ cockleshoreguardian.com."

"Well, fancy you being in the paper Hannah!" said Edward.

Hannah smiled. "I was just about to tell you when Septimus appeared," she said.

"I have an idea," said Edward. "I won't be long!"

He glided through the closed door only to return a few minutes later carrying a large bottle of lemonade. Close behind him followed Mary, Maisie and Horace.

"Congratulations everyone on a very successful mission!" said Edward, raising his glass.

"Oh!" said Hannah. "There is something else I must tell you! The owner of the castle has given me a free pass and told my Mum and Dad he'll look after me when I'm here, so now I can visit whenever I wish!"

"That's splendid news!" said Edward. "Three cheers for Hannah!"

Hannah smiled. "And three cheers for the ghosts of Cockleshore Castle!"

HORACE
AND THE STOWAWAY

A Quick Brown Fox Publications Book

First published in Great Britain by Quick Brown Fox in 2009.
Copyright © Diana Shaw, 2009.

Also by the same author:
Septimus Smythe And The Spectre Detectors
(ISBN 9780955480454)

ISBN-10 0955480493
ISBN-13 9780955480492

Cover Image and Illustrations © Zosia Olenska, 2009.

Cover Design and Image Editing © Chris Goodier, 2009. With
lettering and additional artwork from Nicola Stanton.

Edited by Adam Kirkman.

Quick Brown Fox Publications is an independent publisher.
Why not let them know what you thought of this book?

www.quickbrownfoxpublications.co.uk

HORACE
AND THE STOWAWAY

A GHOSTS OF COCKLESHORE CASTLE STORY

DIANA SHAW

ILLUSTRATIONS BY
ZOSIA OLENSKA

Quick Brown Fox Publications, 2009

Edward looked up from the book he was reading and peered over his glasses at the library clock. Goodness, it was almost time!

Swiftly, he took a shortcut through the middle bookcase. It would not do to be late for the Spectrecise class. Funny, he hadn't heard the bell. Septimus began promptly at eight o'clock every Tuesday evening and woe betide anyone who was not in time for the warm up session!

The Great Hall was buzzing with conversation.

"Have you seen him?" someone asked Edward.

"Seen who?"

"Horace. He's not here. He didn't ring the bell.

He hasn't been seen since about four o'clock!"

Septimus raised his hand and everyone stopped to listen.

"The class will be delayed for half an hour," he announced. "I'm going to the top of the tower to see if there is any sign of Horace."

With that, Septimus glided out through the main doors into the courtyard. He looked up at the tower. A few months ago, he would have found it difficult to reach the top in one glide, but since his holiday away from the castle, he felt fit and strong. Seconds later, he was standing on top of the tower. Down below in the courtyard the other ghosts had gathered, hoping for news of their friend Horace. It was very unusual for one of them to just disappear!

Septimus peered down. The castle grounds were deserted. He looked beyond the drawbridge to the lane leading away, with fields on either side where sheep and cows grazed, but there was no sign of anyone. It was hours since the last visitors had left and the owner of the castle had locked up and driven away. Despite the warm September evening, Septimus felt a little shiver creep over him. The light was fading fast and one of his friends was missing.

He turned towards the sea. About three

miles up the coast, lights were coming on in Cockleshore, a bustling seaside town. Many of the visitors to the castle stayed there on holiday. It was a favourite with the cruise ships, too. They often called in before heading off to more exotic places. Septimus looked at the cruise ship anchored out in the bay now.

He could see the little launch boat as it ferried passengers back from their day out in Cockleshore. He looked down now to where the waves slapped the rocks beneath the tower, sending spray high into the air.

"Horace!" Septimus shouted in relief. Below him on the rocks sat the ghostly sailor gazing out to sea.

"Horace!" Septimus shouted louder but the figure did not move.

He looked down into the courtyard where the other ghosts still waited.

"Horace is on the rocks by the sea. I'll go down to him," he called.

Edward waved to show they had heard him then he led the others back inside the hall to warm up for their Spectrecise class.

Septimus swooped down and landed on the nearest flat rock.

"Horace," he said gently. "Horace, are you alright?"

Slowly Horace turned his head.

"Oh," he said in surprise as if he had just woken up. "Oh, whatever is the time? Have you been looking for me?"

"Sorry if I startled you," Septimus said, "but it's quarter past eight and no-one had seen you for ages! We were all quite worried. Whatever are you doing out here?"

"You know how people get homesick? Well, I'm seasick! No, that can't be right, can it? I mean I'm homesick for the sea! I've not been on a ship since the Albatross ran aground on these very rocks at the time of Good Queen Bess, more than four hundred years ago."

"I remember the night you arrived," said Septimus. "What a stormy night! All wet and bedraggled; you were a sorry sight!"

"You and the others who were here at the time were so good to me. Don't think I'm not grateful. I just fancy going sailing again!" Horace said.

Septimus looked thoughtful. "Ships have changed since you were a sailor though, haven't they?"

"I'll say," Horace replied. "Just look at that monstrosity out in the bay. How could you call travelling on that thing sailing? It was a tough job in my day; always at the mercy of the weather, we were! We relied on the wind

5

to be in our favour and the stars to guide us. But when it was stormy, we could be blown miles off course. Then there were times when we were becalmed; days we spent just floating helplessly with not even a breeze to fill our sails. Nowadays, it's all machines! Even the sailing ships have engines to help them out if the wind drops. Still," he sighed, "I wouldn't mind a sea trip now and then."

"Well then," said Septimus, "what's stopping you? Here we are, close to the sea. You could glide out and have a look at the cruise ship and maybe take a ride in the launch!"

Horace smiled. "You know," he said, "I think I will! You don't mind if I miss the Spectrecise class for once, do you?"

"Of course not," said Septimus. "I'll explain to the others. Off you go and enjoy yourself for an hour or two!"

Horace reached for his crutch and stood up. Despite having just one good leg, he was as agile as could be, balancing skilfully on the wooden peg that served for the other. Now he walked to the edge of the rock where he had been sitting and rose into the air.

"See you soon," he called as he glided off across the bay.

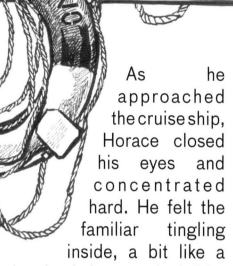

As he approached the cruise ship, Horace closed his eyes and concentrated hard. He felt the familiar tingling inside, a bit like a sneeze starting, as he slowly became invisible. It could be quite tricky for a ghost! When he opened his eyes again, he was near enough to see people walking up and down on the promenade deck, and to hear the chatter of their voices. Somewhere on the ship, lively music was playing.

He was amazed by the size of the craft. Tied up alongside was the launch, so tiny by comparison. He had heard visitors to the castle refer to the cruise ship as a floating hotel. He knew what a hotel was like. He had been inside several. Some of the ghosts had occasionally

made nocturnal visits to Cockleshore for a look around. He remembered the splendid Grand Hotel with its luxurious rooms. Sometimes, dances were held there and you could hear the music playing. But this great ship was many, many times the size of the Grand.

He landed lightly on the deck, almost colliding with a large woman who came blustering round the corner.

"Oh!" she said to the short, thin man beside her, "Where did that icy cold breeze come from? It made me shiver!"

"You must have imagined it," said the man. "It's such a warm evening. I didn't feel anything."

The woman continued to grumble as Horace swiftly moved away.

He floated along the deck, curious to find out where the music was coming from. Passing through a closed door, then down a flight of stairs, he was amazed to find himself in a brightly lit room where people were standing around in groups or sitting at tables chatting and sipping brightly coloured drinks.

In one corner, a string quartet played lively music. Now and then, some people would move through into another room beyond. Horace decided to have a look what was going on through there. The doors were standing open

and as he approached, he could see people seated at tables set for dinner.

At one side of the room was a long table displaying the most sumptuous buffet food. Horace felt his stomach rumble. He just fancied one of those chicken legs as he hadn't eaten since lunchtime!

He joined the queue for the food, taking care not to stand too close to the person in front. He couldn't do with anyone else complaining about the cold sensation his presence created. Just then, the bald man in front of him greedily snatched up the last two chicken legs and put them on his plate.

Horace was so cross he quickly grabbed one of the legs and dived under the table! The bald man swung round to face the large woman who had joined the queue behind him.

"How dare you take my chicken?" he bellowed.

The poor woman was dumbfounded. "I don't know what you are talking about," she said, looking down at the two solitary lettuce leaves on her plate. "I'm on a diet!"

The woman's husband quickly leapt to her defence. "How dare you accuse my wife?" he roared.

Meanwhile, well hidden under the table,

Horace nibbled on his chicken. The tablecloth touched the floor on all sides and he felt confident enough to materialise. Staying invisible for a long time was very tiring and he needed a break from it.

Besides, when a ghost was invisible, he couldn't eat! Otherwise the food would just float about in mid-air. Some ghosts were stuck being invisible: they usually starved to – well, not to death, but something worse.

Above his head, the argument continued until at last someone came along with more chicken and calmed the situation.

"Oh dear, what a fuss," muttered Horace. "I don't want to cause any more trouble. I think I'll get out of here."

Invisible once more, he emerged from his hiding place and dropped the chicken bone on the nearest empty plate, which just happened to belong to the large woman. The bald man saw it, but the woman didn't notice him giving her a very nasty stare.

Horace glided off, not stopping until he was back on deck. It was quite dark now and there was no-one around, so he boldly materialised and ambled along taking in the sea air.

He could see the lights of Cockleshore across the water and he thought about taking a ride on

the launch, but when he looked down, he could see the boat tied up alongside and there was no-one aboard.

For a fleeting moment, he considered sailing the launch himself but the sound of footsteps approaching made him quickly focus his mind on becoming invisible once more. This was all too much and very tiring. Missing today's spectrecise class had made him unfit!

Looking up, he saw a row of lifeboats attached to the side of the ship. He decided to rest in one of those for a while. He floated up and lifted the canvas cover from the nearest boat then climbed inside.

"That's better!" Horace said aloud.

He stretched out in the bottom of the boat as bit by bit he reappeared. What would the people aboard this ship have thought if they could have seen him with his long black hair plaited in a pigtail down his back?

Over one eye, he wore a patch and dangling from his ears were gold hoops. He was dressed in a striped jersey and navy breeches. Now he placed his crutch beside him and made himself comfortable.

There had been one or two close shaves but he wasn't ready to return to the castle just yet. There was so much more to see! He yawned.

Maybe he should just close his eyes and rest for a few minutes before going exploring again...

Down below, on the promenade deck, the large woman and her husband were returning from dinner.

"My goodness!" she exclaimed. "I'm sure I just heard someone snoring."

"There you go, imagining things again," said her husband.

Little did they know that just above their heads a ghostly sailor lay fast asleep!

mussels and mermaids!

Horace woke suddenly. He could hear voices nearby and the sound of many footsteps.

"Where am I?" he asked himself as he fumbled around in the dark to find his crutch. He sat up and bumped into the canvas.

"Oh my goodness!" he exclaimed. "I must have fallen asleep in the lifeboat!"

Cautiously, he raised the edge of the canvas a tiny bit. Daylight streamed in. He had been there all night!

"Mussels and mermaids! I'll have to be getting back to the castle. Septimus and the others will be getting really worried."

Horace concentrated on becoming invisible then glided up through the canvas, not bothering to move it out of the way, and landed lightly

on the deck. It was crowded with passengers, many following their noses to the dining room from where a strong smell of cooked bacon drifted. For a moment, Horace was tempted to join them, but he knew he should go straight home.

He wasn't sure which direction to take, so he decided to glide up to the highest point on the ship to get his bearings.

Oh no! He could see very clearly in all directions, but where was Cockleshore? The little town had vanished along with the rest of the coastline. All Horace could see was the ocean all around him, stretching on for what seemed forever into the distance.

What a predicament! He dare not leave the ship; if he set off in the wrong direction he could get completely lost and never find his way home! It was no good; he would have to stay on board until the ship returned to Cockleshore Bay. He thought about Septimus and the others; they would be worried about him, but what could he do? One thing was certain; right now he felt very hungry. He would grab himself a snack from the dining room and find somewhere out of sight where he could eat it.

One large bacon sandwich later, he settled down on a deckchair overlooking the swimming

pool. He had discovered the sun deck, one
level up from the promenade deck. There were
lots of empty seats as it was still quite early.
If he had to stay on the ship, he might as well
make the best of it, and as long as he remained
invisible, he felt safe. Horace felt the warm sun
beating down. He closed his eyes and dozed...
"Oh! Mussels and mermaids, what's
happening?"
He felt his chair being dragged along from
behind. Quickly he glided up in the air. He was
just in time, for the man who had been moving
the chair now flopped down on it where he had
placed it, nearer to the pool.
Horace looked around. Most of the deckchairs
had been taken now; it was time to move on.
He decided to find somewhere quiet where he
could materialise for a while. Gliding along the
deck, he came to some double doors displaying
signs that read:

Curious, he went inside.

"Knees bent! Arms stretch! Step to the right, one, two, then to the left, one, two!"

Horace found himself standing at the end of a line of people as they all moved in unison. He quickly darted out of the way as the line stepped towards him.

"Mussels and mermaids, it's a Spectrecise class!" he said. "I can do without that right now! My poor old back still feels a bit sore from sleeping in the lifeboat!"

Standing to one side, he watched as a man at the front demonstrated whilst bellowing out his instructions. Horace waited for his chance. As the group stepped forward, he glided neatly behind them across the room.

At the far end were other doors and, passing through, he found himself in a room that seemed to be full of the strangest machines. A woman was walking along on a wide black belt that moved and yet she seemed to travel nowhere! After a few minutes, the belt stopped and then woman stepped off and left the room.

Horace was alone now; he could materialise. The temptation was too great to resist; he stepped onto the belt! Nothing happened. He moved forward and studied the panel on a box in front of him. There were two buttons.

"That's simple enough," he told himself, "green for go and red for stop!"

He reached out and pressed the green button. After a few seconds, the belt began to move, very slowly. He started to walk.

"It must go faster than this," he thought.

Impatiently, he leaned forward and prodded the button several times. The belt began to move faster, and faster and faster!

Poor Horace grabbed the handles on either side and held on for dear life as he broke into a trot and then a run!

His one good foot and his peg leg pounded on the belt as he tried to keep up.

"Stop!" he cried, but of course it was useless to shout.

He could see the red button, just out of reach. If he let go with one hand and leaned forward a little...

Oops! The moment he let go, he lost his balance. Spinning round on his peg leg, he tried to grab the handle again.

It was no good! He could not hold on any longer with just one hand. He skidded along the belt and shot off the end! For a few seconds he was airborne then he crash-landed on a pile of mats stacked up nearby!

"Oh!" he groaned between the puffing and

panting. "Oh! That was worse than being shipwrecked!"

Slowly, he sat up. Apart from his dignity, nothing else seemed to be hurt, so he hopped across to where he had left his crutch then headed for the door.

"That's enough of that!" he grumbled.

He glided along the sundeck, searching for somewhere quiet where he could take a rest from being invisible. He stopped by some doors he hadn't seen before and was just about to investigate when the doors slid open and a group of people stepped through towards him. Horace darted past them through the doorway and was surprised to find himself in a small room, not much bigger than a cupboard.

He turned to go out again, just in time to see the doors slide across to shut him in!

There was a shuddering followed by a peculiar whining noise as the room began to travel swiftly downwards! Horace felt as if he had left his stomach behind on the sun deck!

Before he had time to properly panic, he felt a jolt as the room stopped dead.

As the doors began to slide slowly open, a disembodied voice announced, "You have arrived on 'A' deck."

"A ghost!" cried Horace, as he wasted no time getting out of the mysterious room. Not all ghosts were friendly!

The doors slid shut behind him as he heard the voice say, "Going up!"

He was standing at the end of a long corridor that seemed to go on forever.

There were doors on either side and as he slowly began to move along, he could see that they were all numbered.

"Sixteen," he said, pausing. "I suppose that's as good as any."

He glided through to investigate and found himself in a small cabin. The room was bright and cheerful with a porthole looking out to sea.

There was a single bed and a small wardrobe. At either end of the room were doors. Horace discovered that one led into a tiny bathroom.

He floated through the other to find another cabin, big enough for two people.

Returning to the single bed, he decided to lie down for a while.

All the passengers were out on deck, he felt sure it would be quite safe to materialise...

It was the sound of the door opening that woke him. Too late to become invisible, he sat bolt upright in bed and faced the person who entered.

"Who are you?" asked the boy in surprise. "And what are you doing in my cabin?"

"I'm sorry," Horace said, climbing off the bed. "I must have made a mistake. They all look the same and I was tired."

"But I'm sure Gran locked the door." The boy sounded puzzled.

"Don't worry; I'll get out of your way. I am sorry."

Horace stood up just as a voice from the corridor called, "William!"

Someone was coming!

Horace closed his eyes and concentrated as hard as he could. The rest had done him good. In a second, he was invisible.

"Wow!" he heard the boy say.

The door opened and a woman entered the cabin.

"I thought I heard you talking to someone, William," she said, looking round. "Must have imagined it."

She crossed the room and opened the door leading to the adjoining cabin.

"Anyway, you have a rest for a while; you'll be staying up late tonight!"

"Alright, Gran."

The woman stepped through into the other cabin and closed the door behind her.

Horace was about to leave when he heard William whisper, "Are you still there?"

He stopped, unsure what he should do.

"Please come back," the boy said.

Slowly, Horace materialised.

"Fantastic! How did you do that?" William was sitting on the edge of the bed staring at Horace who had just reappeared in the middle of the cabin.

Horace paused for a moment then said, "I'm a ghost. I hope I haven't scared you."

"A ghost! Well, I suppose you must be. Living people can't vanish like that. Not unless it's a trick."

"It's a ghost trick," Horace said. "I died when my ship was wrecked about four hundred years ago, when Good Queen Bess was on the throne."

"What's your name?" William asked.

"Horace."

"I'm William. You probably heard Gran say. I'm on this cruise with my Gran and Granddad. Mum and Dad had to cancel our holiday this year because Dad moved to a new job, so Gran and Granddad brought me with them for a treat. What are you doing here? Do you haunt the ship?"

"Oh no," Horace explained. "I haunt a castle near Cockleshore. I was exploring the ship when it was anchored in the bay. Unfortunately, I fell asleep and when I awoke, the ship had set sail so here I am! I don't know the way home so I will have to stay until the ship returns to Cockleshore Bay."

William looked Horace up and down carefully.

"Oh, sorry!" he said suddenly. "I didn't mean to stare but I was wondering about your leg. What happened to it?"

"Oh, that!" said Horace. "A shark made a tasty snack of it. One day, a freak wave washed me overboard.

"If it hadn't been for my shipmates, pulling me from the sea just in time, I think he'd have had the rest of me for the main course!"

"That's horrible!" William said, shuddering.

Then he looked thoughtful. "Do you have a cabin?" he asked Horace.

"Not really," said Horace, looking a bit guilty. "In fact, I am finding it quite difficult to find a safe hiding place. I did sleep in one of the lifeboats but it was very cramped."

"I know! Why don't you stay here? I won't tell anyone. There's a spare duvet and some pillows. We can make you a bed on the floor. As long as we don't make any noise, Gran and Granddad won't hear."

"That's really kind of you," Horace said. "I'll try not to be any trouble."

"Good, that's settled then."

William was quiet for a moment then he said,

"I've just had a great idea! You can come to the party tonight!"

"What do you mean?" Horace asked. "I can't possibly let anyone see me!"

"But you can! Tonight, anyway. It's a fancy dress party. Everyone will be dressed up, and you look brilliant!"

CHAPTER FIVE

"What was it like being a pirate?" asked William.

"I'm not sure," said Horace.

"But I thought the skull and crossbones was a special pirate sign."

Horace suddenly realised that William was staring at the top of his head.

"Oh, the hat; now that did belong to a pirate. He was one of a crew who attacked our ship. I was struggling with him when he lost his balance and fell overboard; I was left clutching his hat! I like to wear it when I'm haunting at the castle."

"Just wait 'til you see my costume," said William. He opened the wardrobe then stopped.

"Turn around," he told Horace, "and don't look 'til I tell you!"

Horace turned his back and stood looking out of the porthole. He watched the sun setting on the horizon. The sea was so calm; in his sailing days the Albatross would have just drifted, waiting for a wind to fill her sails. The cruise ship, however, ploughed steadily on, cutting through the water, on course for somewhere he could not imagine.

"Ready!"

William's voice woke Horace from his daydream. He swung round and cried out loudly in surprise.

"Well, mussels and mermaids!"

"William!" a voice called from the adjoining room, "turn that television down please, it's far too loud!"

"Sorry, Gran," he replied, trying to stifle a giggle.

"You look like a real pirate," whispered Horace.

William was wearing a three cornered hat with a skull and crossbones badge. His left eye hid behind a black patch. Over a white shirt he wore a black frock coat. When he raised his left arm, his cuff slid back to reveal not a hand but an evil looking hook! His breeches, rather like

the ones Horace was wearing, were tucked into the tops of knee-high boots which completed his costume. William lunged forward, waving his cutlass in the air.

"It's alright," he laughed as Horace took a step back, "it's not real! Besides, how can you hurt a ghost?"

"There are ways," said Horace, darkly. But William hadn't heard him, he was slashing the cutlass to and fro and admiring himself in the mirror.

"I expect there'll be lots of pirates tonight," said William, "as we're on a ship."

"William," Gran was tapping on the door that led through into the other cabin.

Swiftly, Horace glided into the bathroom and out of sight.

William opened the door and Gran peeped round.

"Oh, you do look good!" she said. "We're not quite ready yet, though. Why don't you go ahead to the disco, I'm sure there'll be lots of children there already."

"Great," said William. "See you at the party later."

The door closed and Horace stepped out from his hiding place.

"Let's go!" William said.

They set off together down the long corridor.

"I'm glad I don't have to be invisible!" said Horace. "It is so tiring!"

They reached the end of the corridor and William stopped before the doors to the strange travelling room. Horace took a step back as the doors slid open and the voice announced, "Going up!"

"I'm not getting in there again," he declared. "There's a ghost!"

William laughed.

"It's alright," he said. "This is a lift that takes you from deck to deck. The voice is a recording of a real person. Anyway, you're a ghost!"

Horace looked doubtful. William stepped inside. Not wanting to be left behind, he followed reluctantly.

The doors slid shut; it was too late to escape now! With a sudden jerk, the lift began to travel upwards.

"You have arrived on the sun deck," announced the voice as the doors slid open. Horace felt relieved as he stepped out ahead of William. A group of children walked past dressed ready for the party. There were quite a few pirates around, just as William had predicted. Some had dressed as characters from books or modern day heroes such as Superman or Dr. Who.

"Look!" said William, "there's the Weasley family from Harry Potter!"

Horace had no idea who all these characters were supposed to be but he just laughed and joined in the fun.

They reached some double doors and passed through behind Alice and a large white rabbit. They found themselves in a darkened room where bright coloured lights flashed and loud music played. All around, people were dancing to the music, making a strange sight dressed in their assorted costumes.

"Goodness!" shouted Horace, trying to be heard above the noise. "Whatever is going on?"

"It's a disco!" laughed William. "A sort of dance to pop music!"

"Pop music?" Horace was puzzled.

"The latest popular music," William explained. "That's Undercover you can hear now, they're my favourite band!"

The music faded and a man's voice announced the next disc to be played.

"He's the DJ," William told Horace. "He picks the music to play."

William and Horace were still standing near the doors and just then, they opened to admit more partygoers. Horace gasped.

"Your Majesty!"

William swung round in time to see Horace performing a sweeping bow before none other than Queen Elizabeth I, accompanied by Sir Walter Raleigh!

"Horace!" William hissed. "It's just my Gran and Granddad dressed up!"

Horace blushed but everyone nearby just laughed and crowded round the newcomers, complimenting them on their brilliant fancy dress which had prompted such a reaction. Horace's embarrassment just melted away and he found himself laughing too.

William was busy talking to his grandparents so Horace moved away, weaving his way between the gyrating dancers towards a quieter corner of the room.

Once again, he found himself near a long table almost sagging under the weight of a sumptuous buffet. People were still putting the food out, but he couldn't resist helping himself to a sausage roll.

"Delicious!" he said to himself, munching his way through it as he stood watching the dancing. He could see William on the far side of the room, standing next to Queen Elizabeth and sipping a glass of lemonade. Horace felt

sure that his friend would join him when he could.

Meanwhile, he was enjoying just watching all the people and not having to be invisible. Just then, the DJ announced that the buffet was ready for anyone who felt hungry.

A few people drifted towards the table. Horace stood in the corner and watched, waiting for his chance to take another sausage roll. He noticed a man, dressed as a clown, piling food onto a plate.

As he moved away from the table, he glanced furtively around then quickly left the room through a single door nearby when he thought no-one was watching.

"Strange," murmured Horace to himself. Everyone else was standing around in the room eating or dancing.

"Horace!" It was William. "Gran and Granddad are dancing," he laughed, "so I've managed to escape!"

Just then, the clown returned without his plate. He promptly picked up another and began to load it with food.

"That's odd," said Horace.

"What's odd?" William asked curiously.

"That man, dressed as a clown; he took a plate of food somewhere and now he's helping himself

to some more. Surely, he's not eaten it already. And what has he done with the plate?"

They watched as the man stood nearby, tucking into the second plate of food.

Just then, the DJ announced another Undercover number. William squealed with excitement, "This is their new song! It's called Super Sonic Stereo, and it's my favourite! Come on, Horace – dance with me!"

William began to dance around wildly to the music whilst Horace – who hadn't danced for four hundred years – did his best to join in, jogging up and down on the spot in a most peculiar manner.

William laughed at his friend so much that the strange clown was forgotten.

Horace understood that he and William could not spend much time together. It would not do for his Gran and Granddad to get curious about him. Now and again, William would dance nearby with some other children and have a chat with his friend.

"Time for the judging of the fancy dress competition," he told Horace as the disco was ending.

Everyone stood around the sides of the room. The captain of the ship had been asked to announce the winners. He was a tall man

with a bushy grey beard and a spotless white uniform.

He stepped up to the microphone as the DJ handed him a piece of paper. There were several prizes for children and adults; Alice and the white rabbit won a prize, as did Elizabeth I and Sir Walter.

"Finally," the captain said, "for our overall winner, we've chosen the sailor with the peg leg. I'm not sure how you have managed to keep your leg tucked up in your breeches all evening, but well done!"

Horace felt a gentle push from William as the people standing nearby began to clap. He stepped forward into the spotlight and received a large box of chocolates from the captain.

"Thank you," he said, and then moved away quickly before anyone could ask any awkward questions.

"See you back in the cabin later for a feast," whispered

William, eyeing the chocolates with a large grin.

Clutching his prize, Horace headed for the single door. Before he could pass through, he almost collided with the suspicious clown who was coming the other way, carrying an empty plate. Horace watched as the clown placed the plate on the table and quickly passed back through the doorway. He followed him out in time to see him remove the bright orange wig to reveal a mop of black hair.

"Time to become invisible," Horace said to himself and he concentrated as the tingling sensation began. He hid the chocolates in a dark corner to collect later and then set off along the corridor after the clown.

"Oh no! Not another of those lift things!" Horace muttered to himself as the clown stopped suddenly and pressed a button on the wall. Horace reluctantly followed him inside and felt his stomach lurch as the lift travelled down; he was relieved to hear the disembodied voice announce that they had arrived back on 'A' deck.

They had not gone far when the clown came to a halt outside a cabin. He paused and looked around before unlocking the door and stepping inside.

"Number sixty," Horace made a mental note. It was quite a long way from William's cabin.

He heard the key turn as the man locked the door behind him. That was no problem. Horace just glided through the closed door into the cabin.

"You ok?" The clown was speaking to a young man with spiky hair who was sitting on a chair in the corner.

"Sure," he replied. "No-one's been near."

"Not long to wait now," the clown said. He disappeared into the bathroom.

Horace glided back through the door and along the corridor once more.

"Now what was all that about?" he said to himself. "Why is that man hiding in the cabin? I must go and tell William."

He made a quick detour to collect his prize – using the stairs this time – then he went to William's cabin.

As they steadily munched their way through the top layer of chocolates, Horace described all he had seen and heard while his friend listened carefully.

"You know what I think?" said William after a while. "I think he's a stowaway! Something strange is going on and we're going to find out what!"

Horace woke early. William was still asleep so he decided to go for a stroll. He concentrated on becoming invisible before he left the cabin and then he headed for the promenade deck. Still unhappy about using the lift, he glided up the stairs and was surprised to find many people heading the same way.

"That's odd for so early in the morning," he said to himself.

He stepped out onto the deck. People were lining the rail chattering and pointing in excitement. Horace found a gap and glided through. What a surprise; he could see land!

"Majorca," someone said. "Can't wait to visit Palma!"

"The launch starts to ferry people across straight after breakfast," said one of the crew who was passing.

Horace felt excited. He really fancied a trip in the launch, it was much more like real sailing than being on this huge ferry. And it had been four hundred years since he'd set foot on foreign soil!

"Majorca, Palma," he said the names to himself. "Sounds fun! I must go and tell William!"

He was in so much of a hurry that he just took the nearest stairway without thinking about whether it was the right one. Down he glided to A deck, but he found himself at the wrong end of the corridor. The first cabin number he read was seventy-two. Slowly, he began to make his way along then suddenly, just ahead of him, a door opened.

Horace thought he recognised the man who emerged from the cabin. Of course, he wasn't wearing the clown suit any more, but there was the mop of black hair he had seen when the wig was removed. The man locked the door and walked to the lift.

Horace couldn't resist a peep inside the cabin. The man with the spiky hair was standing by

the porthole, talking to someone on his mobile phone.

"Mike's on his way now," he was saying. "He'll meet you outside the cathedral at two o'clock as arranged. See you tonight!"

"So the other man is called Mike," Horace thought to himself. "It sounds as if he is going to meet someone. I wonder where the cathedral is."

Horace couldn't wait to tell William what was going on. Hopefully, he would know where the cathedral was.

"Sixty, fifty-eight, fifty-six... forty-two, forty... twenty-three, twenty-two... eighteen, sixteen!" he counted the cabins as he whizzed along the corridor.

When William came out from the bathroom, he found the ghost sitting on his bed.

"Horace! Where have you been?" he asked.

"Doing a bit of invisible detective work," Horace replied.

He went on to tell William all about what he had seen and heard.

"Sounds strange; so you think the clown man, Mike, has gone off on the launch? Well, Gran and Granddad are taking me over on the next one. It leaves in half an hour. I've never been here before so I don't know where the cathedral

is but I'm sure we can find it. I think you'd better come too and we'll try to find out what's going on."

Invisible once more, Horace grabbed a round of toast from the dining room. He had to materialise to eat it so he hid behind a curtain until he had finished, and then he joined the queue for the launch. He could see William a little way ahead. He waited until the last passengers were boarding then glided on behind them. The seats were all taken, so he glided up onto the roof of the small cabin where the pilot sat.

"Whee! What fun!"

As the launch sped across the water, he felt the spray on his face as it splashed up the front of the boat. The smell of salty air filled his lungs. This was more like it! Horace felt quite disappointed as the launch tied up at the landing stage; he was already looking forward to the sail back!

"Just look at the cathedral!" exclaimed someone seated below him.

Horace could see the magnificent building towering over the city. It would certainly be easy to find!

He waited until he saw William and his grandparents leave the launch, then swiftly

glided after them along the streets crowded with tourists. They came to a square surrounded by cafés where tables with bright sun umbrellas were set out across the pavements.

"Whew! It's hot!" said William's Gran, "I think we'll stop for a drink before we do any sightseeing."

"May I go and see the fountain?" asked William. In a corner of the square, only a short distance away, water splashed down from a fountain into a pool beneath. The spray sparkled like jewels in the sunlight. Laughing children splashed in the shallow pool as passers-by tried to dodge a soaking.

"Yes, but stay where we can see you."

William wandered over and stood where he could feel the cooling spray on his face.

"Are you there, Horace?" he whispered, hoping that no-one would notice a boy talking to himself.

"Yes," said Horace. "That was a great trip on the launch wasn't it? I've been thinking; I can be on the cathedral steps at two o'clock to see what Mike is up to."

"Good. I'm not sure where we'll be at that time. Make sure you don't miss the launch back!"

"I wouldn't miss it for the world!" grinned Horace.

¡CHAPTER EIGHT!

The first thing Horace did was to make sure he could find his way to the cathedral, and then, with two hours to go to Mike's meeting, he decided to do some sightseeing of his own. Palma was an exciting place with lots going on and plenty to see.

"What's going on over there?" Horace wondered.

A group of tourists had gathered on a corner and they seemed to be very interested in something. Weaving in and out between the people, Horace made his way to the front of

the crowd. He was surprised to see a statue of a man dressed in long robes. The statue shimmered in the sunlight, for every bit of it was painted silver; even his face was silver!

Suddenly, the woman next to Horace shrieked and jumped backwards, bumping into the man behind her.

"He winked at me!" she cried.

Someone burst out laughing and others joined in, but their laughter turned to surprised cries as the statue suddenly came to life! The silver man stepped down from the platform where he had been standing and from beneath his robes he produced a small collecting box which he held out to the crowd. Realising they had been fooled, most people good humouredly dropped coins into his box before moving on. Horace chuckled to himself.

"What fun," he thought. "I might be able to use a trick like that at the castle!"

He glided up a little side street until he came to another square. All around the edge and arranged in rows across the square were stalls shaded with brightly coloured canopies. Horace wandered from stall to stall captivated by the atmosphere of the market. A colourful assortment of vegetables and fruits of every kind adorned some of the stalls. Horace

followed his nose to a stall where wedges of cheese and slices of cured meat cut from long sausages were weighed out to order. Oh, how his mouth watered!

He was beginning to feel hot, tired and hungry now so he made his way to the beach and sat down in the shade of a bright red umbrella, next to a man reading a newspaper. As the man turned a page, Horace suddenly noticed something. There was a picture of five men and the man in the middle looked remarkably like the spiky-haired stowaway!

Horace tried to read what it said next to the picture. There were lots of words in bold print and several exclamation marks, but it was all written in a foreign language he could not understand.

Just then, two children came running up the beach as a woman appeared from the direction of a little snack bar, carrying a bag. Horace had to move quickly to avoid being sat on! He watched from a safe distance as the woman handed round sandwiches.

His poor stomach rumbled; it was one o'clock and all he had eaten that day was the round of toast for breakfast. How was a ghost supposed to do important detective work on an empty stomach?

He knew it was wrong but he could not resist it; when no-one was looking, he reached over and took one of the four sandwiches that remained. It was ham and cheese, his favourite! He would have to make himself visible to eat it, so he hid it inside his coat until he could get away. Just then, he was aware of raised voices.

The woman was handing round the remaining sandwiches and had discovered there were not enough. She waved her arms, gabbling away in the strange language and pointing towards the snack bar.

"Oops! Time for me to go!" said Horace to himself. He could see an argument brewing.

Back in the square, he washed down his sandwich with a long, cool drink of water from the fountain before setting off for the cathedral. If anyone had noticed a funnily dressed man eating a sandwich they hadn't said anything!

He arrived at the cathedral early as he didn't want to miss Mike.

He found a shady spot where he had a good view of the steps and settled down to wait. He could see a clock on a building nearby; at five minutes to two, a tall, fair-haired man wearing sunglasses walked past. He looked oddly familiar...

He stopped at the foot of the steps and looked

around, then raised his hand in recognition. Horace could see Mike approaching; not long to wait now!

The men stood chatting for a few moments inside the cathedral, then set off walking down a narrow street. Horace swiftly followed. Suddenly, they stopped outside a house, glanced quickly up and down the empty street, then disappeared inside.

It took a few moments for his eyes to adjust to the dullness after the bright sunlight outside, but what Horace saw next took him completely by surprise.

There were three other people in the dingy room and, together with Mike's companion, he recognised them as the four standing with the stowaway in the newspaper photograph!

"I left Jason in the cabin," Mike was saying. "He was going to have a look around the ship once most of the passengers had come ashore. You four must sail across separately. When you get on board, make for the theatre; there is a little room at the back of the stage. We will meet up there."

"Do you think we'll make much tonight, boss?" one of the men asked.

"I'm sure of it," said Mike. "The passengers will turn up for the usual show but they'll get a

surprise when they see you all. They won't be able to resist handing over their money!"

"Oh! Mussels and mermaids!" thought Horace. "I know what their game is. They are modern-day pirates! They are going to rob the passengers on the cruise ship! I'll bet that picture in the newspaper is a 'Wanted' poster. Whatever can I do?"

"Right, you take the next launch," Mike was telling the man he had met on the cathedral steps. "Wear your sunglasses and keep your hat pulled well forward. It's vital that you are not recognised!"

As the man left, Horace decided that he must follow. He would return to the ship straight away and find out all he could to tell William. He was so worried about the pirates that he didn't enjoy the sail back!

Back on board the cruise ship, Horace watched as the man he had followed headed straight for the theatre.

"Better see what Jason the stowaway is up to," he thought.

He glided along to cabin sixty and passed through the closed door. Jason glanced at his watch and reached for a pair of sunglasses. He checked his appearance in the mirror, then started for the door.

Before he could reach it, however, Horace swiftly removed the key.

"Hey! What's going on?" shouted Jason in alarm as he watched the key floating.

"You're not going anywhere!" Horace cried and with that, he began to materialise. First, his head began to appear, with his pirate hat perched on top of Horace's scariest face. Septimus would have been proud! Finally, his peg leg appeared with a clunk on the ground. Poor Jason, overcome with fright, stumbled backwards onto the bed.

"W-w-where did y-you come from?" he stammered, his face white with fear.

"I just appeared," declared Horace. "I'm a ghost, you see. I come and go as I please."

"B-b-but I don't believe in ghosts," said Jason, covered in confusion.

"Well, believe it or not, here I am. Furthermore, I know what you and your gang are up to!"

"Gang? What are you talking about?" Jason had stopped shaking and now he just sat looking at Horace with a puzzled expression.

"I heard Mike and the others talking. You're going to take money from all the passengers when they go to the theatre tonight! Well, your game is up. You're locked in here and I'm off to fetch the police!"

Chapter
Nine

"Hey! Wait a minute!" shouted Jason as Horace began to disappear. "You've got it all wrong!"

"What do you mean?" asked Horace, stopping mid-vanish with only the top part of his body still visible. "I saw your picture in the newspaper. You and your gang are wanted by the police!"

To Horace's surprise, Jason burst out laughing!

"Oh no!" he spluttered, trying to control his laughter. "That was a publicity picture of me with the rest of the band. I don't suppose a ghost would have heard of Undercover!"

"Undercover?" said Horace, "Well, as a matter of fact, I have! I was dancing to their music at the discotheque!"

"Imagine," chuckled Jason. "A ghost dancing to Undercover; just wait 'til I tell the boys!"

"I don't see what's so funny about that," said Horace indignantly, "ghosts can dance you know!" The rest of his body began to slowly reappear.

"Sorry," said Jason. "I didn't mean to offend you."

"Hmm. Well, you have five minutes to explain what all this secrecy is about. You have to admit it looks mighty suspicious!"

"You're right, it does. There is to be a big charity concert in Palma and Undercover is top

of the bill. It has all been a secret until today, when an article advertising the event appeared in the newspaper; that was what you saw!"

"Well, why have you been hiding like a stowaway?" Horace asked.

"Our appearance at the concert was to be a surprise. I decided to travel separately from the rest of the band so no-one would guess we were on our way to a gig. I couldn't wander about the ship in case I was recognised. It's actually been pretty boring, stuck here in my cabin."

"But that doesn't explain why the rest of your band is, at this moment, hiding on the ship, waiting to take money from the passengers tonight," said Horace.

"Take money, yes, but it is all for charity! We thought we would do a special extra performance for the passengers. The ship sails before the concert in Palma so they wouldn't be able to come."

"Hmm, it all sounds as if it might be true." Horace thought for a moment. "I know how to resolve this once and for all!" he said suddenly. "If you really are from Undercover then my friend William will recognise you, he's a big fan! I will go and bring him here."

"Agreed! If William is a fan of Undercover then

he should recognise me and you'll soon know I'm telling the truth!"

"Back soon," said Horace, still clutching the key; with that, he quickly vanished. He glided along the corridor to William's cabin. Bursting in through the closed door, he looked around for his friend, but William wasn't there!

"Oh no! They're not back yet!" he cried.

He set off for the deck and arrived just as the launch was tying up alongside. He watched the passengers as they transferred from the little boat to the cruise ship. Thank goodness! He could see William and his grandparents. He was just about to follow them when he spotted Mike coming aboard.

"Oh no! If he goes straight to the cabin it could cause problems," Horace thought. "Just say they really are criminals; they could get clean away before I could do anything!"

He decided to follow Mike. Fortunately, he headed straight for the theatre. Horace followed him into the little room.

"Good," Mike said to the three people who were waiting there. "When Pete arrives on the next launch I'll fetch Jason."

There was no time to lose. Horace sped off to cabin sixteen where he was lucky to find William alone.

"Quickly!" he panted, without bothering to materialise. William nearly jumped out of his skin.

"Where are you?" he asked. "You scared me!"

"Sorry, but we must go now. I want you to meet someone. Go to cabin sixty and wait outside."

"Why? What's going on?" William asked, but there was no reply. There was nothing else he could do but go to cabin sixty.

William opened his cabin door and looked up and down the corridor. There was no-one around. He would just have to risk his Gran finding him missing. He walked along to cabin sixty and stood looking at the closed door. What next?

Without warning, the door opened. There stood Horace and, beside him, a tall man with spiky hair.

"Jason Brown!" William cried out in disbelief.

"Hi, William!" Jason turned to Horace. "Well?" he said.

"Alright. I'm satisfied," Horace said.

"I think we had better explain all this to William, don't you?" said Jason, looking at the boy's bewildered expression.

It didn't take long for the star-struck William to be brought up to speed.

"Well," said William after he'd listened to the story. "You can't blame Horace for being suspicious. Your manager Mike acted very strangely at the disco and you have been hiding away in this cabin for the whole journey!"

"Yes, I'm sorry about that. But everything had to be kept a secret! I must ask you to keep our secret about Undercover for just two more hours. In return, I will make sure that there are

three reserved seats on the front row for you and your grandparents."

"That's great, thank you!" William said, and then added, "but what about Horace? He should be able to watch the concert, too."

Jason thought for a moment.

"I know!" he said suddenly. "The captain is the only one who knows the secret apart from you. Mike can ask him to tell the passengers that tonight is a gala concert and would everyone please come dressed in the costumes they wore for the disco. That way, Horace does not need to be invisible and I get to see all the costumes!"

"Can he sit on the front row too, please?" William asked.

"Of course!" said Jason. "I'll speak to Mike. Now off you go and get ready. See you later!"

"I wonder why we were given such good seats," said Gran as they all waited for the concert to begin.

"I can see the sailor with the wooden leg a bit further up," said William. "Perhaps it's because you all won prizes at the disco."

Just then, the captain walked onto the stage.

"Good evening, everyone. Thank you for wearing your costumes. As you may have guessed, something special is happening tonight. Here, for one time only, we are delighted to welcome the hit band Undercover!"

For a moment, the audience sat in silent disbelief. Then the curtains opened and Undercover leapt onto the stage. The air exploded with the sound of clapping and

cheering as Jason Brown stepped forward to sing. The first number was Super Sonic Stereo, the band's latest hit, and everyone joined in! Some people even danced in the aisles!

The band played some of their best songs and William sang along to every single one. Horace even began to enjoy himself! When it was time for their last song, Jason raised his arm to speak.

"We're glad you are all enjoying yourselves," he said. "This is our last song, after this we're going to move to the disco so we can all dance. We'd just like to dedicate this to two very special fans – to William and Horace!"

The audience clapped their approval and Undercover played a brand new song. William had a huge grin from ear to ear!

The rest of the evening was fantastic. Everyone danced and danced at the disco until well after midnight. Horace was never far away from William who could not help laughing at his friend's antics as he spun round and round on his wooden leg!

At the end of the evening, people were more than happy to hand over their money for charity and over ten thousand pounds were raised. People were leaving and William was walking

behind his grandparents when he felt a tap on his shoulder. Turning, he saw a smiling Jason who handed him a special photo signed by all the band members! William's Gran couldn't understand why but was happy for him!

The next morning, a crowd gathered to wave to Undercover as the launch ferried them back to Palma. William waved and cheered and so did Horace but no-one could see him! When the launch was too far away for them to see the band anymore, people drifted off to the dining room for breakfast.

Horace helped himself to a couple of rounds of toast then returned to William's cabin to wait for him. Lying on the table was the photograph of the band. Horace picked it up and looked at it.

It had certainly been a fantastic evening and Horace was so glad that Jason hadn't been a real stowaway. Oh dear, what if he had sent for the police, he daren't think about it!

"What are you dreaming about?" William asked as he entered the cabin.

"I was thinking about the band and the great time we had," said Horace.

"Yes," William agreed. "Wasn't it good; our own special concert! And we even got a song dedicated to us!"

There was silence for a moment.

"What happens next?" asked Horace.

"The ship sails today," replied William. "There's another week of cruising before we return to Cockleshore Bay."

"Well, let's enjoy it then," said Horace. "I'm really looking forward to seeing my friends at the castle again, but in the meantime the rest of the cruise should be fun!"

"Jason said you can use his cabin. It will be empty for the rest of the trip. You can have a proper bed to sleep on!" laughed William.

"That," said Horace, rubbing his sore back and scratching his peg leg, "would be very welcome!"

Early one morning, exactly one week later, William sneaked out to the promenade deck to meet Horace. They stood together by the rail, looking out across the water at the coastline they were approaching.

"Cockleshore," said Horace. "Home again!"

"We've had a great time," said William, then he added a little sadly, "will I ever see you again?"

"Of course! You can come to the castle on a visit and I'll introduce you to all my friends."

"Next time we come to Cockleshore!" laughed William. "I promise."

William's grandparents decided to spend the day relaxing on the sundeck rather than taking the launch to Cockleshore. William was glad because Horace had decided not to return to the castle until the evening so that they could spend some time together. Many passengers did go ashore so there were quiet areas where Horace could materialise for a while. While Gran and Granddad snoozed under a sun umbrella, William was allowed to go off and play so he and Horace had fun playing deck quoits and exploring the ship.

All too soon, evening came and it was time for Horace to go. He went along to William's cabin to say goodbye.

"Remember to visit," he said.

"Don't worry, I will!"

William watched as his ghostly friend shut his eyes and concentrated hard then suddenly vanished.

"Goodbye," said a voice as a cool breeze blew gently past William, and Horace was gone.

William stood gazing out of the porthole for a while. He could not see Horace but he imagined him gliding away across the sea to the castle on the rocks.

It was dark when Horace reached the castle. He glided through the heavy doors and landed in the middle of the Great Hall. It was deserted; everyone must have gone to bed. Horace quickly materialised. He could not wait until morning to see his friends. There was nothing else for it: he would just have to wake them! He crossed the room to the little table on which rested the ancient ship's bell salvaged from the Albatross. With no further thought, he picked up the bell and began to ring it!

Septimus was first on the scene.

"Whatever is going on; is the castle on fire?" he asked, rubbing his eyes. Then he saw his friend.

"Horace!" he cried in excitement. "Come quickly everyone; Horace is home!"

From every corner of the castle came all the other ghosts, every one of them delighted at their friend's safe return.

"We guessed what had happened when we realised the ship had sailed," said Septimus. "Well, Horace, looks like you got your wish, didn't you? Did you enjoy your sea trip?"

Horace smiled. "I'll say. I made a new friend called William and we went to a disco. We visited Majorca and I thought there was a stowaway on the ship and..."

Septimus raised his hand. "Hang on a minute. This sounds as if it could take some time," he laughed. "Edward, why don't you put the kettle on? Then we can all settle down to listen with a nice cup of tea..."